Boo to You Too!

For my mother, Mary Rodger, M.B.E., J.P.,
with my love and thanks for always being there,
and for the many happy memories of Halloween

First Troll edition published in 2002.

Copyright © 1993 by Elizabeth Rodger.
Published by Troll Communications L.L.C.
Printed in the United States of America.   ISBN 0-8167-7591-5
10 9 8 7 6 5 4 3 2 1

Boo to You Too!

Elizabeth Rodger

Halloween was coming.

The Pig family went to buy the biggest pumpkin they could find.

"You deserve the biggest because you're such wonderful children," Father said to Sally, Toby, and Charlie.

There were many pumpkins of all different sizes.
The Pig children rushed back and forth looking
at this pumpkin, looking at that pumpkin.
    Then Sally squealed. "I've found it! Look over here!
It's the biggest pumpkin ever!"

But Sally didn't know someone was hiding behind the big pumpkin.

"*Boooooo!*" shouted Charlie, the littlest pig, as he jumped from his hiding place.

But Sally just laughed.

Charlie didn't look scary at all.

At home, Father Pig helped carve a face in the pumpkin. The face had a friendly grin.

Charlie didn't like that. The friendly grin was not scary enough for Halloween.

Well, he would just have to show them.

Charlie made a mask out of a paper bag. He put
the mask over his head.

"*Boooooo!*" he shouted, jumping out from behind a door.

But Toby just laughed.

Charlie was too little to be scary.

The Pig family talked and giggled as they
tied pillows on a stake to make a ghost.

The ghost looked very plump dressed in a long,
white sheet.

It's not a very scary ghost, thought Charlie.

Well, he would just have to show them.

Charlie pulled a white sheet over himself.
Not even his little toes showed.

Making what he was sure were creepy moans,
he tiptoed behind his family.

But Charlie couldn't see where he was going.
He stumbled over a bush. He stubbed his toe
on a root. He bumped into a tree.
Ouch! Down he fell to the ground.

Mother tried to comfort Charlie.

"I want Halloween to be scary," huffed Charlie.

"But Halloween is scary," said Toby. "Just you wait and see."

Then Halloween came.
The little pigs put on their costumes.
They were so excited! They could hardly wait to go
from door to door filling their bags with all sorts of goodies.

Mother and the children were ready to leave.

Charlie looked at the darkness all around. Things looked different from before. The big pumpkin was grinning in a spooky way and the ghost looked eerie in the moonlight.

Shadowy figures lurked here and there. Ghostly lights
blinked through the tall trees.

Charlie held on tightly to Mother's hand.

What fun to go from house to house trick-or-treating!
Molly Possum gave them candied apples.

Bebe Mouse had baked tiny pecan tarts. She gave two to each little pig.

Even grumpy Gramps Badger had plenty of fudge to put in their bags.
Soon the bags were filled with goodies.

Mother and the children went back home.

There they found the pumpkin glowing in the dark and the ghost where they had left it.

Suddenly, Charlie saw the ghost move. But how could that be? The ghost was just a stuffed sheet.

Then it moved again.

"Look! Look!" squealed Charlie. "The ghost moved! It moved its arm!"

Mother, Sally, and Toby stopped to look. The ghost didn't move.

"Don't be silly, Charlie. It's just an old sheet stuffed with pillows. Now come along, dear," said Mother.

Charlie was sure the ghost had moved.
He kept an eye on it as he trotted after
his mother.

Then the ghost moved its leg. Charlie stopped to look more closely. The leg moved again.

"Look! It did it again! It really did move!" squeaked Charlie.

"Oh, you're just imagining things," said Mother.
She walked up to the ghost and poked it.
   The ghost didn't move.
   "There! Now you try, Charlie," said Mother.

Ever so slowly, Charlie put out a hand.
He gave the ghost a quick little poke
in the middle of its very round tummy.

"*Boooooo!*" roared the ghost as it pounced on Charlie and swept him up in its great white arms.

Charlie squealed and squealed.

He was so scared!

Mother, Sally, and Toby began to laugh.
The ghost was laughing, too.
What was going on?

The ghost raised its hood. There was Father's happy face grinning at Charlie.

"Gotcha! Boo to you too!" said Father, hugging Charlie.

Charlie giggled. What fun it was to get
a big scare on Halloween.
Now it was a perfect Halloween.